HA! HA!

TO ALL THE CHILDREN WHO SHARED THEIR WORRIES WITH ME. THANK YOU.

LAUGH AT A WORRY TODAY.

First published 1990 by Walker Books Ltd
87 Vauxhall Walk, London SE11 5HJ

© 1990 Marcia Williams

Printed in Hong Kong by
South China Printing Co. (1988) Ltd

British Library Cataloguing in Publication Data
Williams, Marcia
Not a worry in the world.
I. Title
741
ISBN 0-7445-1539-4

NOT A WORRY IN THE WORLD

MARCIA WILLIAMS

WALKER BOOKS
LONDON

Every now and then,

when I've nothing better to do,

I start to worry.

I worry that Mum will turn off the light…

before I get to sleep,

or that I'll dream I'm falling off a cliff again…

I worry that my family will be so busy

playing with my sister or doing other things

that they will forget my birthday

and I won't have a party or presents.

I worry that the woman next door is a witch
and she will take me up to the clouds and leave me there.

I worry that Mum will forget

to pick me up from school,

or that my teacher will ask me something tricky.

GOOD-BUYS SUPERMARKET
FOR ALL YOUR FAMILY NEEDS

I worry that I'll get lost in the supermarket,

or that my sister will be wheeled away by a stranger.

I worry about going to a party…

dressed in the wrong clothes.

I worry that the animals will escape from the zoo!

Every now and then, when I've nothing better to do,

I worry about all these things.

Sometimes I worry so much

that I bite my nails,

or even … suck my thumb!

Every now and then a worry comes along

which won't go away…

for days and days and days.

But I've found out the secret of worries –

they can't stand being talked about.

It makes them so mad

that even the worst worries run away.